SUPER PARROT

For Cathy

First Steck-Vaughn Edition 1992

Copyright © 1989 American Teacher Publications

Published by Steck-Vaughn Company

Library of Congress number: 89-3552

Library of Congress Cataloging in Publication Data.

Benitez, Mirna.
  Super parrot.

  (Real readers)
  Summary: Polly the Parrot hitches a ride on Carmen's hat with surprising results.
[1. Parrots—Fiction]. I. Banek, Yvette Santiago, ill. II. Title. III. Series.
PZ7.B43455Su 1989 [E]   89-3552

ISBN 0-8172-3503-5   hardcover library binding

ISBN 0-8114-6704-X   softcover binding

4 5 6 7 8 9 0 01 00 99 98

Super Parrot

by **Mirna Benitez**

illustrated by **Yvette Banek**

RSVP

RAINTREE STECK-VAUGHN
P U B L I S H E R S
The Steck-Vaughn Company

Austin, Texas

Carmen has a parrot. The parrot's name is Polly. Polly has green feathers. She has red feathers, too.

"Get up, Carmen!" says Polly when the sun comes up.

"Feed me, Carmen!" says Polly when she wants to eat.

Polly can sing, too. She sings when Carmen sings.

"There was a man who had a dog," sings Carmen.

"There was a man who had a parrot," sings Polly.

"No, no, Polly," says Carmen. "He had a dog, not a parrot."

Polly can tell jokes.

"What is green and red, has a cape, and can fly?" she says.

"I don't know," says Carmen.

"Super parrot!" says Polly.

Carmen laughs. Carmen's mom and dad laugh, too.

Carmen is going to sing in a big talent show. Lots of boys and girls will sing, do tricks, and tell jokes in the talent show. Carmen hopes that she will win.

Carmen's mom makes a big green hat for Carmen. The hat has green and red feathers on it.

Carmen puts on the hat. She sings, "And Bingo was its name-O!"

Polly sings, too, "And Polly was its name-O!"

"No, no, Polly," says Carmen. "The dog's name was not Polly! It was Bingo."

It is time to go to the talent show. Carmen puts the hat with green and red feathers in a bag. She does not see Polly get in the bag. Polly's feathers look like the feathers on the hat.

Carmen thinks about singing in the talent show. "I hope that I will win," thinks Carmen.

It is time for the talent show. Carmen puts on the hat with the green and red feathers. Polly is on the hat, but Carmen does not see the parrot.

"Carmen will sing 'Bingo,'" Kim says.

The boys and girls see the parrot on Carmen's hat. They laugh at Polly.

"What is going on?" thinks Carmen. Then she finds out about Polly. It is too late to take the parrot home.

"There was a man who had a dog," sings Carmen.

"There was a man who had a parrot," sings Polly.

"And Bingo was its name-O!" sings Carmen.

"And Polly was its name-O!" sings Polly.

The boys and girls laugh and laugh.

Carmen stops singing. Now Polly tells a joke.

"What is green and red, has a cape, and can fly?" the parrot says.

"We don't know," say the boys and girls.

"Super parrot!" says Polly.

The boys and girls laugh and laugh. They fall off the seats.

Carmen and Polly go home.

"Did you win?" says Carmen's mom.

"I did not win a thing!" says Carmen. "But Polly did win. She made the boys and girls laugh and laugh. They fell off the seats."

"Are you a good parrot, Polly?" says Carmen's mom.

"Super parrot!" says Polly.

Sharing the Joy of Reading

Beginning readers enjoy reading books on their own. Reading a book is a worthwhile activity in and of itself for a young reader. However, a child's reading can be even more rewarding if it is shared. This sharing can enhance your child's appreciation— both of the book and of his or her own abilities.

   Now that your child has read **Super Parrot**, you can help extend your child's reading experience by encouraging him or her to:

- Retell the story or key concepts presented in this story in his or her own words. The retelling can be oral or written.

- Create a picture of a favorite character, event, or concept from this book.

- Express his or her own ideas and feelings about the characters in this book and other things the characters might do.

Here is a special activity that you and your child can do together to further extend the appreciation of this book: You and your child can make medals, like the one Polly won in the talent show. Discuss with your child things that you are each very good at. (For example, Your child might be very good at riding a bike, or drawing.) Cut medal shapes out of pieces of colored construction paper. Use a crayon to write what the medals are for on the shapes (for example, #1 Bike Rider). Decorative touches can be added with markers or crayons or by glueing on ribbons and glitter. Finish the medals by sticking a loop of tape in the back. Then you both can wear your medals.